Published by Parragon in 2011

Parragon
Queen Street House
4 Queen Street
Bath BA1 1HE, UK

DUMBO

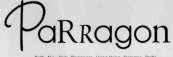

Bath · New York · Singapore · Hong Kong · Cologne · Delhi
Melbourne · Amsterdam · Johannesburg · Auckland · Shenzhen

Early one morning, a flock of storks flew over the countryside, carrying little bundles of joy for the animals waiting below.

A circus was on its way to town, and Mr. Stork landed on the roof of the train car.

'Special delivery for Mrs. Jumbo!' he called, hopping from one train car to another.

Suddenly, he saw several elephant trunks waving at him from the elephant car.

'Yoo-hoo! Yoo-hoo! In here!' the elephants called.

Mr. Stork hopped into the train car.

'Which one of you ladies is expecting a little bundle of joy?' he asked.

'Right over there,' the elephants answered, pointing to Mrs. Jumbo.

She smiled shyly as Mr. Stork placed the bundle at her feet, cleared his throat and began to recite, 'Here is a baby with eyes of blue, straight from heaven—right to you!'

'Do hurry, dearie,' the other elephants urged as Mrs. Jumbo began to untie the bundle with her trunk.

'Oooh!' everyone cooed when the bundle fell open. For there sat an adorable baby elephant, with a sweet little trunk, and big blue eyes.

Mrs. Jumbo decided she would call him Jumbo Junior.

'Kootchy-kootchy-koo!' one of the elephants said, tickling the baby under his chin.

'Aaachoo!' the little elephant sneezed. His ears, which had been tucked behind his head, flopped open. They were enormous!

The other elephants shrieked with laughter.

'With ears like that, you should call him Dumbo!' one elephant giggled.

The elephants teasing made Mrs. Jumbo angry. She didn't care if her baby's ears were big, she thought he was beautiful just the way he was.

The next morning, the circus arrived in town. Little Dumbo trotted behind his mother in the parade.

'Look at the adorable little baby elephant!' the townspeople said.

Mrs. Jumbo and her baby made their way to the elephant tent. Suddenly, some rowdy boys found their way inside.

'Look at those ears!' the boys laughed. 'Isn't that the funniest thing you ever saw?'

The boys wiggled their ears, and stuck out their tongues at Dumbo.

Dumbo tried to hide behind his mother, but the boys wouldn't leave him alone. Laughing and jeering, they crawled behind the ropes and pulled his ears.

Mrs. Jumbo wanted to protect her baby. She picked up a bale of hay, and threw it at the boys, trying to scare them away.

'Help! Mad elephant!' the boys cried, and ran away, screaming.

The Ringmaster dashed into the tent.
'Down, Mrs. Jumbo!' he shouted, cracking his whip in the air.

Then someone tried to pull Dumbo away. Furious, Mrs. Jumbo bellowed and charged.

'Wild elephant! Wild elephant!' the townspeople cried, running in all directions. Animal trainers threw ropes around Mrs. Jumbo, who fought and strained against them.

But Mrs. Jumbo was no match for the men and their strong ropes. At last, she was too exhausted to fight anymore.

'Lock her up,' the Ringmaster commanded.

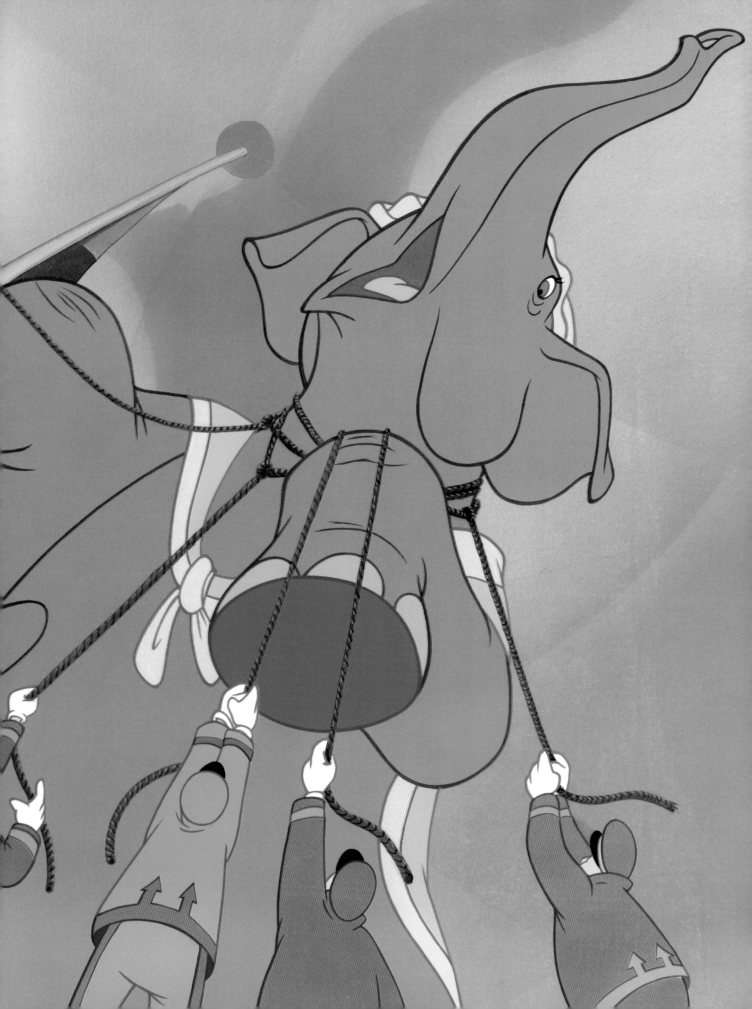

As Dumbo watched, the trainers dragged his mother away. They locked her in a wagon that was set apart from the rest of the circus.

There, with her legs in chains, Mrs. Jumbo stood weeping for her baby.

Poor little Dumbo was left all alone. He crept over to the other elephants, hoping they would help him. But they turned their back to him. 'Mrs. Jumbo's behavior is a disgrace, and it's all his fault!' they said.

Ignored by the other elephants, he felt as though he didn't have a single friend in the whole world.

But Dumbo was wrong. Someone did want to be his friend.

In the corner of the tent, sat a little mouse named Timothy.
He had been watching the whole time, and had seen and heard
everything. When Timothy saw how the other elephants treated
Dumbo, it made him mad.

'Look at the poor little fella,' the mouse said. 'Everyone's making
fun of his ears. What's the matter with them? I think they're cute.'

'I'm going to do something about this,' Timothy decided. He
swaggered into the midst of the gossiping elephants and made a face.
'So you like to pick on little guys,' he said. 'Well, why don't you pick on
me, you bunch of hay bags?'

The elephants bellowed in fear and backed away from the brave
little mouse.

'They're all afraid of a mouse,' Timothy laughed. 'Wait till I tell the little guy.' But Dumbo was scared of Timothy, too. Timothy found him hiding beneath a pile of hay.

'Aw, you aren't afraid of little old me, are you?' Timothy asked. 'I'm Timothy Mouse, and I'm your friend, Dumbo. I have a plan to help you free your mother.'

At that, Dumbo forgot all about being scared. He crawled out of the hay and listened wide-eyed to everything his new friend had to say.

'I know you're embarrassed by your ears, kid,' Timothy said. 'But lots of people with big ears are famous. So all we gotta do is make you a big star. But first we need a really colossal act.'

That night, as the Ringmaster slept, Timothy sneaked into his tent. He crawled under the sheet and crept close to the Ringmaster's pillow. Timothy whispered his idea into the Ringmaster's ear.

The very next day, the Ringmaster stepped into the spotlight. 'Ladies and Gentlemen,' he announced. 'We will now present the most magnificent event ever seen! On this insignificant ball, we will construct an elephant pyramid!'

Dumbo and Timothy watched as the pyramid rose higher and higher, until it almost reached the top of the tent.

'And now, Ladies and Gentlemen,' the Ringmaster shouted, 'the world's smallest elephant will spring to the top of the pyramid!' Drums rolled and trumpets blared. A bright spotlight shone on Dumbo. He froze with stage fright.

'You can do it, kid,' Timothy said, nudging Dumbo. Startled, Dumbo ran to the springboard. But before he could make his leap, his ears came untied. He tripped over them and went sprawling headfirst into the elephant pyramid.

For a moment, the stunned crowd watched in silence as the elephant pyramid teetered and swayed. Then they ran for their lives as the elephants began to fall.

Trumpeting and bellowing, the elephants tumbled down, crashing into beams and platforms and bleachers. They smacked into walls and pulled down wires and ropes. Finally, they crashed into the center tent pole.

After the damage was cleared up, the elephants decided they never wanted to work with Dumbo again.

'You won't have to!' one elephant said, 'they have made him into a clown!'

The very next show, the clowns painted Dumbo's face and dressed him as a baby. They put him on a tiny platform high up in a building surrounded by crackling, make-believe flames.

'The baby will have to jump!' the clown firechief announced. The firemen held up a thin safety net. Closing his eyes, Dumbo leaped from the building.

Dumbo fell through the net and landed in a tub of wet plaster. The audience roared with laughter.

As the clowns bowed to the cheering crowds, they paid no attention to Dumbo, who crept from the tent feeling hurt, humiliated, and miserable. After the show, the clowns celebrated in their tent.

'Cheer up, Dumbo,' Timothy said as he scrubbed his friend's sad little face. 'I've found out where they're keeping your mother. I'm going to take you to see her later tonight.'

A wistful smile crossed Dumbo's face. Things wouldn't seem so bad if he could just see his mother.

'Cheer up
Dumbo.'

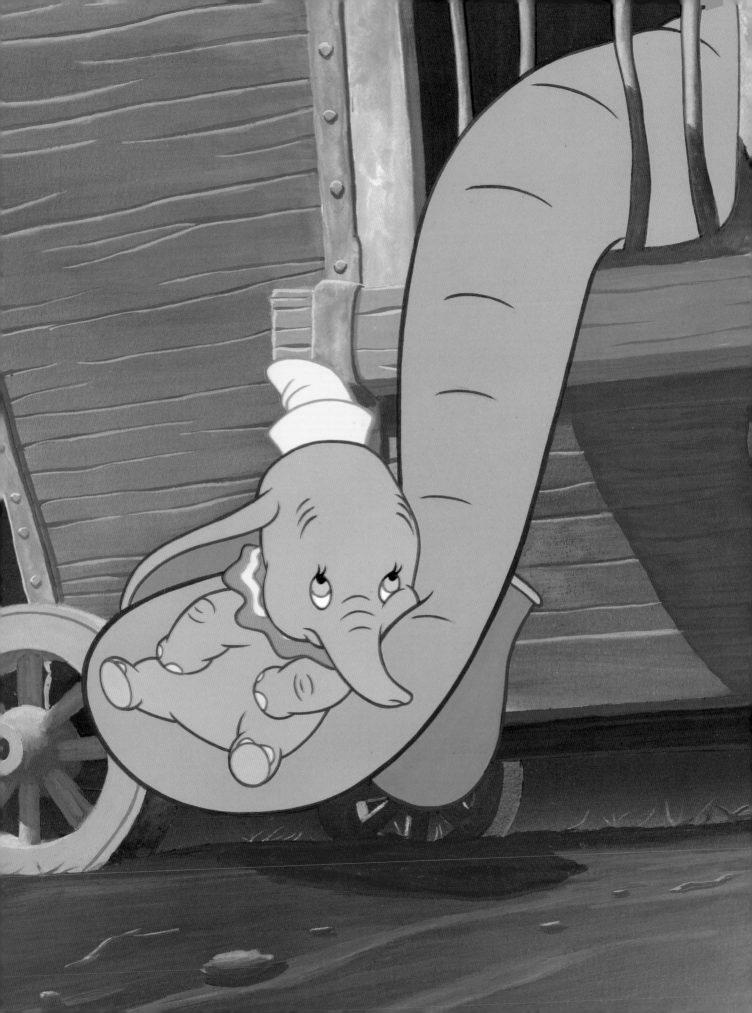

Later that night, Timothy took Dumbo to the wagon where his mother was chained.

'Mrs. Jumbo, someone to see you!' Timothy called.

Mrs. Jumbo put her trunk through the bars of the window and stroked Dumbo's head. She wrapped her trunk around Dumbo and rocked him lovingly.

At last it was time to leave. Tearfully, Dumbo and his mother waved goodbye.

As Timothy and Dumbo returned to the clowns' tent, they heard the clowns talking about their act.

'Aw, you can't hurt an elephant. They're made of rubber!' One clown waved his hand scornfully. No one noticed that in his excitement, he knocked a bottle into Dumbo's tub.

That night, Dumbo and Timothy had some very strange dreams...

As dawn broke, a flock of crows perched on a tall tree stared at the strangest sight they'd ever seen. There on a branch, high above the ground, a little elephant lay sleeping peacefully. And in his trunk was a mouse. It was Dumbo and Timothy. 'We'd better wake those two up and find out what they're doing here,' the crows decided. 'This is our tree. Elephants don't belong up here.'

'Maybe they flew up?' One of the crows suggested.

Timothy stared at Dumbo's ears. 'That's it, Dumbo!' he exclaimed. 'Your ears! They're perfect wings! You're the world's only flying elephant!'

One crow plucked a shiny black tail feather and gave it to Timothy. 'Tell the little guy that this is a magic feather,' the crow said. 'As long as he holds onto it, he can fly.'

Dumbo clutched his feather, closed his eyes, flapped his ears, and suddenly he was soaring.

'You're really flying!' Timothy shouted. 'I knew you could do it! Wait till the next performance. We'll show everyone what you can do!'

Soon it was time for Dumbo to perform again with the clowns.

'Boy, are they in for a surprise!' Timothy chuckled as Dumbo jumped from the platform. But as they flew through the air, the wind tore the feather from Dumbo's trunk. Dumbo froze. Without his magic feather, he didn't believe he could fly. He and Timothy hurtled toward the ground.

Timothy slid to the end of Dumbo's trunk. 'Open your ears and fly!' he pleaded. 'The magic feather was just a gag. You can fly all by yourself!'

Dumbo heard Timothy's words and believed them. And what's more, he believed in himself. At the last second, Dumbo spread his ears, soaring up and up and up.

The astonished audience went wild as Dumbo zoomed after the clowns, chasing them around the ring. The crowd roared as he dove at the Ringmaster. They applauded thunderously as Dumbo did loop-the-loops and rolls and spins in the air.

Dumbo was famous. By the next morning, every newspaper carried pictures of him and Timothy. 'Wonder Elephant Soars to Fame,' the headlines screamed. In every village, town, and city, people flocked to the circus to see Dumbo, the flying elephant.

Dumbo thought it was great fun being a star. But what he loved best of all...was being with his mother once again.